Vol. 166 No. 41 ★ ★ ★ Thursday

RED TAPE HOLDS UP NEW BRIDGE

AND MORE FLUBS FROM THE NATION'S PRESS

Edited by Gloria Cooper | Collected by the Columbia Journalism Review

A Columbia Journalism Review Book

Library of Congress Cataloging-in-Publication Data

Red tape holds up new bridge, more flubs from the nation's press

1. Errors and blunders, literacy. 2. American newspapers–Language.
3. Newspapers–Headlines. 4. American wit and humor.
I. Cooper, Gloria. II. Columbia journalism review.

PN 6231.B8R4 1987   070.4´44´0973   87-16755
ISBN 0-399-51406-6

Printed in the United States of America
                    6 7 8 9 10

Errare humanum est.

Literarcy week observed

Brandenburg, Ky., *Messenger* 9/4/85

Never Withhold Herpes Infection From Loved One

Albuquerque Journal 12/26/84

Warranty aids home owners with defects

Knoxville (Tenn.) News-Sentinel 3/18/80

All-Stars turn on sparse crowd

The Southfield Eccentric (Birmingham. Mich.) 8/11/83

In England, Trials Quick and Efficient

Los Angeles Times 12/20/85

Reader is upset over dog eating Filipinos

The Wayne County Outlook (Monticello, Ky.) 2/25/82

Rhode Island secretary excites furniture experts

The Star-Ledger (Newark, N.J.) 6/2/87

Hunter Dies; Deer Count Holds Steady

Daily News-Record (Harrisonburg, Va.) 11/18/82

Man Is Seized in Burglaries By Use of a Pool Skimmer

The New York Times 8/25/85

Correction

The band Raging Saint base their music on born-again Christian principles. They are not "unrepentant headbangers," as reported in the Night life column last Friday.

Austin American-Statesman 3/10/87

Dartmouth Names Computer Vice Provost

Valley News (White River Jct., Vt.) 3/10/86

More of us will live to be centurions

The Times Reporter (Dover-New Philadelphia, O.) 2/11/87

Smaller home wave
is expected in future

Sun Herald (North Olmstead, Ohio) 5/6/82

Police brutality postponed

The Mishawaka (Ind.) Enterprise 10/1/81

Reagan goes for juggler in Midwest

The Charleston (W. Va.) Gazette 11/3/84

3 U.S. firms bomb targets in Spain

Chicago Sun-Times 1/6/86

Despite our best efforts, black employment is still rising

The Evening Times (West Palm Beach, Fla.) 10/3/80

Morality rates lower than normal at Mobil

Woodbury, N.J., *Gloucester County Times* 6/10/85

Police said they had to bring him to the ground twice before they confiscated the pistol from a pants leg.

"I would describe it as hairy," said Sgt. Lou Daliso who, with Officer Tom Green, wrestled the suspect.

The Reporter Dispatch (White Plains, N.Y.) 3/15/81

8 U.S. soldiers die in Grenada

Idaho delegation pleased

Idaho Press-Tribune 10/26/83

Services for man who refused to hate Thursday in Atlanta

(Detroit) *Michigan Chronicle* 11/17/84

Retired priest may marry Springsteen

Bloomington, Ind. *Herald-Times* 5/12/85

Defendant's speech ends in long sentence

Minneapolis Tribune 2/25/81

Mondale's offensive looks hard to beat

Anchorage Times 12/23/83

Associated Press

Kicking Baby Considered to Be Healthy

The Burlington (Vt.) Free Press 9/18/80

Silver Objects Often Taken — Police Units Seek Pattern

The New York Times 2/16/86

British left waffles on Falklands

The Guardian 4/28/82

How to combat that feeling of helplessness with illegal drugs

The Royal Gazette (Bermuda) 5/9/85

Grover man draws prison term, fine for sex acts

San Luis Obispo, Calif., *Telegram-Tribune* 6/3/84

Obituaries
Area

Ms. Michelle **O'Brien**, 39. of Wistar Village Drive, a tired employee of Richmond Newspapers Inc.

Richmond Times-Dispatch 11/25/79

Fried chicken cooked in microwave wins trip

The (Portland) *Oregonian* 7/8/81

Belfast man charged for Harrods bomb

Chicago Tribune 3/23/84

City's First Mayor To Be Born in Cuba

The Washington Post 11/13/85

Humans Are Joining Native Trout's Fight to Survive in a Nearby Stream

The Washington Post 2/13/84

Four county liquor stores sold to teen

The Montgomery Journal (Montgomery County, Md.) 8/8/84

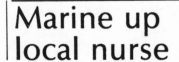

Marine up local nurse

Dearborn Hts. (Mich.) *Leader* 12/29/83

Air Force considers dropping some new weapons

New Orleans *Times-Picayune* 5/22/83

U.S. banks wrestle with Argentine deb

Duluth *News-Tribune & Herald* 3/29/84

Health officials warn some meningitis non-fatal

Port Arthur (Tex.) *News* 7/3/83

Chef throws his heart into helping feed needy

Louisville Courier-Journal 11/22/85

Kampala. — A hand grenade exploded on board a passenger train killing a Uganda Army soldier who was toying with it and two civilian passengers.

The (London) Times 3/27/82

Late bus coordinator remembered

New London, Conn., Day 4/10/85

Reagan raps need to prove sanity

The Oregonian 7/2/82

Wimbledon Gentlemen Get Their Wish

The Post-Journal (Jamestown, N.Y.) 6/29/82

Prison warden says inmates may have 3 guns

The Idaho Statesman 1/11/85

Sharks Stop Search for Span Collapse Victims

Seattle Post-Intelligencer 5/11/80

Coach Suspended In Sexual Probe; Players Honored

Daily Press (Newport News, Va.) 12/15/81

Israelis Withdrawing From Beirut

Marines Poised To Enter

The Pittsburgh Press 9/27/82

19 Feet Broken in Pole Vault

Wichita (Kan.) Eagle-Beacon 6/21/81

Amusements

Princess Grace's brother shot

Fort Worth Star-Telegram 12/29/82

Life means caring for hospital director

Hamilton, Ont., Spectator 8/20/85

Rebel threats keep traffic light in El Salvador

The Atlanta Journal and Constitution 1/20/85

5½-foot boa caught in toilet; woman relieved

The Sun-Tattler (Broward County, Fla.) 1/25/84

Johnson
Teacher Talks
Very Slow

Indianapolis News 8/9/82

Henshaw Offers
Rare Opportunity
To Goose Hunters

San Diego Union 12/25/80

Disappearance of 4 workers baffles police

St. Petersburg Times 4/6/86

Would she climb to top of Mr. Everest again? Absolutely!

Houston Chronicle 12/8/80

Gates asks Reagan to recall name

Daily Iowan 3/3/87

Obscene snow sculptures built by two fraternities Chi Psi and Delta Upsilon, had aroused townspeople as well as the administration.

Addison Independent (Middlebury, Vt.) 3/15/79

W. Germany disagrees with sanctions

The Morning Call (ALLENTOWN, PA.) 12/31/8

Sandinistan defends regime in Sioux Falls

Richmond Times-Dispatch 3/16/84

Babies are what the mother eats

The Times-Herald (Newport News, Va.) 7/11/84

Man shot in back, head found in street

Worthington, Minn., *Daily Globe* 12/08/84

Newspaper to recieve seven awards

The Sentinel Ledger (Ocean City, N.J.) 4/7/83

New Quebec premier follows dad's footsteps

Rochester, N.Y., *Times-Union* 10/4/85

WITH MALE DIRECTOR

League of Women Voters Aims To Shed Drag Image

WASHINGTON (AP) — The League of Women Voters, bolstered by a new leadership that includes a forceful president and its first male director, says it is ready to shed its drab image and wants to become America's leading citizens' group by the 1990s.

The Meadville (Pa.) Tribune 7/8/86

Westinghouse Gives Robot Rights to Firm

The Washington Post 6/12/87

Holsteins talk of the winter fair

Brantford (Ont.) Expositor 11/17/83

Jobless Assist Swells

The Times Argus
(Barre-Montpelier, Vt.) 6/2/84

Garden Grove resident naive, foolish judge says

Orange County, Calif., *Register* 7/2/85

Flier to duplicate Miss Earhart's fatal flight

The New Jersey Herald 1/9/84

Jane Weinberger has been married to Casper Weinberger, now secretary of defense, for some 40 years

Crowds Rushing To See
Pope Trample 6 To Death

Journal Star (Peoria, Ill.) 7/9/80

Fashions Shown
to Fight Cancer

Century City, Calif., *News* 6/5/85

Red Tape Holds Up New Bridge

Milford (Conn.) *Citizen* 7/12/82

Man Survived
17 Days Adrift
on Flying Fish

Los Angeles Times 7/11/86

FORMER PRESIDENT
ENTERS DINAH SHORE

The Desert Sun (Palm Springs, Calif.) 3/28/80

Give the Palestinians a homeland -- Ottawa

Toronto Star 7/31/82

Some fossils said to back creationism

Chicago Sun-Times 12/16/81

Baby Safety Week Stresses Parents

The Wichita Eagle-Beacon 9/10/86

Hi, I'm home Unfortunately, missing hunter was supposed to be dead

Everett Herald (Seattle, Wash.) 2/11/80

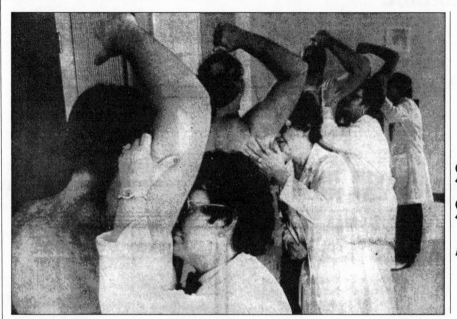

Soviets Will OK Some On-Site Arms Inspections

Honolulu *Star-Bulletin* 8/19/86

13% of U.S. adults unable read or write in English

Times Union (Albany, N.Y.) 4/21/86

Man Held in Fire at His Psychotherapist's Home

Los Angeles Times 1/8/82

Fuel for city buses passes through two middlemen

Detroit Free Press 5/15/82

Experts: Body
Josef Mengele

North Adams, Mass., *Transcript* 6/22/85

Herschel only human in pro debut

The Miami Herald 3/7/83

Threatened by gun, employees testify

The Messenger (Athens, O.) 6/19/84

Legal aid advocates worry

Sunday Pantagraph (Bloomington, Ill.) 6/28/81

Dishonesty policy voted in by Senate

Ball State Daily News 2/8/85

Guyer's widow rules out plans to replace him

The (Cleveland)
Plain Dealer 4/28/81

Vitamin E prevents blindness

igh
soon
prevent
results
ammon
abies
in-

et-
e-
g

quency has increased dra-
matically in the past dec-

Tri-Valley Herald (Livermore, Calif.) 12/3/81

'Mild' fertility drug produces quadruplets in 3 minutes

The (Santa Fe) New Mexican 6/14/81

Religion Plays Major Part In the Message of Easter

Omaha World Herald 4/22/84

Terminal smog not lethal

Valdez (Alaska) Vanguard 8/6/80

Don't go overboard on funerals

Rocky Mountain News 11/3/83

Here's How You Can Lick Doberman's Leg Sores

Reading (Pa.) Eagle 5/23/82

Obscenity Should Include Violence

The Asheville (N.C.) Times 3/21/84

Youths steal funds for charity

The Reporter Dispatch, White Plains, N.Y. 2/17/82

Baseball Talks in 9th Inning

Philadelphia Daily News 5/22/80

Sisters reunited after 18 years in checkout line at supermarket

Arkansas Democrat 9/29/83

Idaho group organizes to help service widows

The Idaho Statesman 3/30/82

Child molesters indicted

Scandal closes day care center

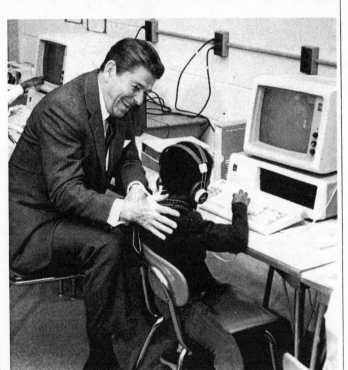

U.S. Press 4/4/84

UPI

Exploding commode floods Poland

A toilet pipe that blew up "like a fire hydrant" shot ankle-deep water across the seventh floor of Poland Hall at about 9 last night.

College Heights Herald (Bowling Green, Ky.) 10/8/85

Eye drops off shelves

Tri-City Herald (Pasco, Wash.) 8/5/82

Pesticide Concerns Blossom

Williamsport, Pa., *Sun-Gazette* 5/21/85

LAST FORMATION — John Peterson (left), Cave Junction police chief, gathers four members of his force outside headquarters. A severe budget crisis will force the department to go out of business Oct. 31.

The Portland *Oregonian* 10/31/80

TV Trashy, Right Wing Mediocre, Says Sociologist

Berkeleyan (University of Calif.) 3/27/85

Correction

The Pacific Rim column in yesterday's BusinessExtra section should have read that Fine Boys is a leading Japanese fashion magazine for guys, not gays. The Chronicle regrets the editing error.

San Francisco Chronicle 2/18/87

U.S approves right to vote for released Texas felons

Houston Chronicle 10/1/83

A Sexual Evolution — Not Revolution

San Diego Union 10/27/80

Prehaps the cruelest tragedy in the death yesterday of James E. Dever is that had it happened a few minutes later, he might still be alive.

Chester County, Pa., *Daily Local News* 1/9/85

good life

SECTION C, THURSDAY, JANUARY 20, 1983

Watt says environmentalists like Nazis

The Oregonian 1/21/83

Sanger (Calif.) Herald 1/20/83

Sharon to press his suit in Israel

East Oregonian (Pendleton, Ore.) 1/25/85

SHUTTLE PASSES TEST; A WORKER IS KILLED

The New York Times 3/20/81

Setting the Record Straight

Last Sunday, The Herald erroneously reported that original Dolphin Johnny Holmes had been an insurance salesman in Raleigh, N.C., that he had won the New York lottery in 1982 and lost the money in a land swindle, that he had been charged with vehicular homicide but acquitted because his mother said she drove the car, and that he stated that the funniest thing he ever saw was Flipper spouting water on George Wilson. Each of these items was erroneous material published inadvertently. He was not an insurance salesman in Raleigh, did not win the lottery, neither he nor his mother was charged or involved in any way with a vehicular homicide, and he made no comment about Flipper or George Wilson. The Herald regrets the errors.

The Miami Herald 12/23/86

Gisèle Berger, in the kitchen of La Bonne Table, with a display of the raw materials she uses for her innovative seafood specialties.

Did Pope suspect plot to murder the Queen?

The Miami News 5/19/81

Police seek woman's Id

The Highland Parker
(Highland Park, Mich.) 10/18/79

New Law Has CHP Officer Jumping for Joy

Lieutenant Who Lost Legs Is Exempted From Physical Agility Test

Los Angeles Times 9/23/83 First edition

New Law Is Leap Forward for CHP Officer

Lieutenant Who Lost His Legs Wins Exemption From Agility Test

Los Angeles Times 9/23/83 Second edition

Sexual misconduct alleged at city hall

The Edmonton (Alberta) *Journal* 9/24/86

PICTURE Bruce Edwards

Dismemberment killer convicted

> " Thank God the jury could put the pieces together.
> — Solicitor Jim Anders

Brockton, Mass., *Enterprise* 8/9/85

Buildings sway from San Francisco to L.A.

The Cleveland Press 5/27/80

UPI photo

Bay residents bid farewell to 'summer'

The Tampa Tribune 1/4/83

Cause of AIDS found—scientists

The Sacramento Union 4/24/84

CORRECTION

■ The Jumble puzzle, which appeared on page D1 of Thursday's edition, actually was the puzzle scheduled to appear today. The Jumble originally scheduled to appear Thursday as well as the answers to Wednesday's puzzle are on page E1 today. The answers to the puzzle published today appeared Thursday, and the answers to the puzzle published Thursday will appear Saturday.

The Arizona Republic 9/28/84

West Greene Busing Plan Draws Fire

Observer Reporter
(Washington, Pa.) 1/22/82

Prince Andrew takes Koo peasant hunting in Scotland

The Atlanta Journal and Constitution 11/28/82

Review Definition of Death, Body Advises

The Japan Times 9/3/85

African gorilla organization talks with Christian accent

Journal-Review (Crawfordsville, Ind.) 9/3/83

She said the man sat on the benches in only his boxer shorts for about five minutes, and exposed himself.

"It wasn't long, but it was long enough," Mrs. Mankin said.

The Star-Democrat (Easton, Md.) 7/1/82

State prison guard suspended for distributing KKK literature

The Vidette Messenger (Valparaiso, Ind.) 6/21/80

Homosexual Loses Boy Scout Suit

The Press-Courier (Oxnard, Calif.) 7/8/81

Potential witness
to murder drunk

Adirondack Daily Enterprise (Saranac Lake, N.Y.) 1/17/85

Singapore addicts
turn to dried dung

San Francisco Examiner 5/11/85

Fuqua school giving up

Cash contributions and pledges to Duke University's Fuqua School of Business Annual Fund increased 120 per cent last year from 1984.

The Durham (N.C.) *Sun* 2/6/86

More Dogs Bring Complaints

Martinsburg, W.Va., *Evening Journal* 10/17/84

Research fans hope for spinal injuries

The Vancouver Sun 7/23/86

Jail guard probed in inmate sex

Chicago Tribune 6/20/86

Kontakis is found guilty of murdering wife after brief deliberation

Somerset (N.J.) *Spectator* 10/17/85

French offer terrorist reward

The Denver Post 11/20/86

Nation's Economy A Mystery, Spaghetti Costlier

Winchester, Ind., *News-Gazette* 6/21/85

Downtown hogs grant cash

Chicago Tribune 2/25/87

Man minus ear waives hearing

Jackson, Tenn., *Sun* 5/26/85

Police kill man with TV tuner

The Blade-Tribune (Oceanside. Calif.) 6/3/86

● There is something more boring than baseball ... Ellen Goodman's column, **Page A-11.**

Roanoke (Va.) *Times & World-News* 7/23/81

Palmy retirement for Jerry Ford

The Milwaukee Journal 2/9/83

Juanin Clay portrays the Lone Ranger's romantic interest.

Fairfax Northern Virginia Sun 6/26/80

Excess of vitamins harmful, expensive specialist warns

London Free Press (Ontario, Canada) 6/22/80

Honduran military chief quits saying he is fatigued

The Daily Journal (Caracas, Venezuela) 1/31/86

"Medical Ethics are the choices we make based on our value system or moral considerations in the field of medicine. The symposium will help people develop principles to make decisions. One example is youth in Asia. You have got the choice of letting a person live on a machine or pulling the plug. What's right?

South Dakota State University
Collegian 3/5/86

Half of U.S. High Schools Require Some Study for Graduation

Los Angeles Times 8/10/81

'Nagging' wife critical after hammer attack

Trenton (N.J.) *Times* 9/2/82

Panty pests easy to control

Oconto County, Wis., *Reporter* 8/8/84

Smokers are productive, but death cuts efficiency

Belleville, Ill., *News-Democrat* 10/25/84

Blind Woman Gets New Kidney From Dad She Hasn't Seen In Years

The Alabama Journal 4/4/84

Jacksonville pornography free, officials say

Tri-City Herald (Pasco, Wash.) 12/16/80

Police Discover
Crack in Australia

International Herald Tribune 9/10/86

Canadian economist feels
rates have hit there peak

The Calgary (Alberta) *Herald* 4/14/80 (first edition)

Canadian economist feels
rates have hit thier peak

The Calgary (Alberta) *Herald* 4/14/80 (second edition)

Haig shuttling to Argentina to defuse crisis

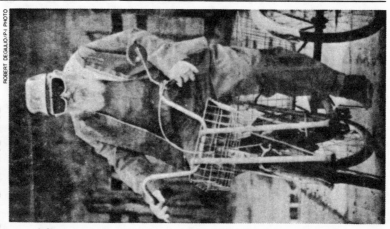

ROBERT DeGULIO/P-I PHOTO

Seattle Post-Intelligencer
4/15/82

Mom ponders approach to sexually active son

The Champaign-Urbana News-Gazette 5/8/84

The new British Library—sitting comfortably on enlarged piles

New Scientist 3/27/86

Workers Accused of Selling Stamps To Be Burned

High Point (N.C.) *Enterprise* 2/4/83

Bundy beats latest date with chair

The Denver Post 11/18/86

Ancestors of apes, humans may have originated in Asia

The Atlanta Constitution 8/16/85

Dr. Ruth Talks About Sex With Newspaper Editors

Rutland (Vt.) Herald 4/14/86

Margiotta is the Sailors most recent recipient of the pretentious Con Edison "Athlete of the Week" Award.

The Croton-Cortlandt (N.Y.) News 1/20/83

Italian gunmen shoot typsetter by mistake

The Philadelphia Inquirer 9 3 80

The Salt Lake City Track Club's All-Women's 10,000-meter race is scheduled Saturday at 8 a.m. at Sugarhouse Park. The entry fee is $4 with shirt or $1 without.

The Salt Lake Tribune 8/27/81

Apartment owners whipping boys

Kitchener-Waterloo (Ont.) Record 6/8/84

A backlash against gays as parents

The Philadelphia Inquirer 7/21/85

White House Kills Fund Raiser
After Complaints About Tactics

Newsday 3/19/81

Old Bridge restricts
outdoor water use;
2 plants break down

The Central New Jersey Home News 5/20/86

More bad mushrooms

NEW BRITAIN, Conn. (AP) — Five more persons were charged Wednesday in the mushrooming investigation of alleged corruption in New Britain's city government, state police reported.

Greenwich Time 11/15/79

CITY PACTS FIGHT BOILS

Chicago *Sun-Times* 8/30/84

British Aide Says All Inmates To Gain Now That Fast Over

The Hartford Courant 10/5/81

Residents were shocked each time their neighbors went on a murder spree

San Francisco Chronicle 12/15/82

By Associated Press

Secretary of State George Shultz, en route to Tokyo with President Reagan, took a dip at a Honolulu beach yesterday morning

'VERY JUICY TARGET'

San Francisco Chronicle 4/28/86

Dog's not always man's best friend

Morning News and Evening Journal (Wilmington, Del.) 9/29/83

Correction

In last week's issue of Community Life, a picture caption listed some unusual gourmet dishes that were enjoyed at a Westwood Library party for students enrolled in a tutorial program for conversational English. Mai Thai Finn is one of the students in the program and was in the center of the photo. We incorrectly listed her name as one of the items on the menu. Community Life regrets the error.

Pascack Valley (N.J.)
Community Life 2/25/81

Large church plans collapse

Hamilton, Ont., *Spectator* 6/8/85

State speeding up welfare cheat checks

Knickerbocker News (Albany, N.Y.) 1/14/82

His humming rear end is a major distraction

The Toronto Star 1/6/86

Blacks Counted Better In 1980

Peoria (III.) Journal Star 4/5/82

Jerk Injures Neck, Wins Award

The Buffalo News 4/6/83

Woman off to jail for sex with boys

The (Kitchener, Ontario) Record 10/23/84

Beg Your Parden

The Daily Progress (Charlottesville, Va.)
3/20/86

Aʙᴏᴜᴛ the *Columbia Journalism Review*

The *Columbia Journalism Review* was founded by Columbia University's Graduate School of Journalism in 1961, "to assess the performance of the press in all its forms, to call attention to its shortcomings and strengths . . . to help stimulate continuing improvement in the profession, and to speak out for what is right, fair, and decent." Today, the *Review* is recognized as the most prestigious journal in the field, attracting a loyal following of some 32,000 readers that includes reporters, editors, news directors, newscasters, and publishers across the country.

From the beginning, the *Review's* most popular department has been the collection of journalistic bloopers that appears under the title "The Lower case." Nominations for this dubious distinction, submitted by readers here and abroad, pour into the editorial offices of the *Review* at an average rate of 300 per issue; of these, a dozen or so make it into print.

This book, published at the suggestion of countless fans, presents some of the choicest flubs from "The Lower case."

Gloria Cooper is managing editor of the *Columbia Journalism Review*.